Research and Rescue

Temerity One

**CALUMET
EDITIONS**

Minneapolis

FIRST EDITION 2024

Research and Rescue: Temerity One, Copyright © 2024 Jennifer Pollard

All rights reserved.

For information, write to:

Calumet Editions

6800 France Avenue S., Suite 370, Edina, MN 55435

10 9 8 7 6 5 4 3 2 1

Cover by Gary Lindberg with AI assistance
Cover and book design: Gary Lindberg

ISBN: 978-1-962834-11-7

Research and Rescue

Temerity One

Jennifer Pollard

CALUMET EDITIONS

Minneapolis

To T.Mike, the most wonderful
husband on Earth.

Chapter One

The wolves gambol in the light rain, gusty wind ruffling their coats. Tem watches from downwind behind some just-budding bushes. Last year's grass has mostly flattened to the ground, revealing patches of ancient road like black and gray rocks poking out of the ground. The gray skies mute what little color early spring offers.

It is necessary to be silent, ignoring the rain, hoping one wolf might come closer by accident and perhaps be willing to communicate. If it stays away from Bunnybun and Squiggles. They are hiding in the backpack, weighing on slight shoulders, frightened into near immobility with the smell of the wolves. The scent is like the smell of wet dog but wilder somehow, a bit rancid and mixed with the smells of the plants breaking dormancy, the storm approaching, and natural composting of last year's greenery.

There are no trees, old walls, or ruins near enough to seek shelter in if a wolf should decide to be unfriendly. Trees line the opposite hillside leaving the shallow valley nearly bare. Maybe it had been cleared of trees long ago for the road now in remnants, and something kept them from moving back in. Maybe pollution from the road and the oil-burning cars that used it had poisoned the soil before the collapse?

It is obviously dangerous to be here. Matron Constance would pop a few blood vessels if she knew. So why tell her and get her all upset? This is better. We get to go on our excursion and do an experiment, maybe add a friend or two, and she gets to stay calm. Plenty of other kids to keep her busy. She doesn't have time for older kids, anyway. When not in class, most of us over ten years old help with the youngers, go visit the elderly next door or help in the gardens and farms. But somehow, the "people" gene seems to have skipped some of us. Or at least one…

Matron will need medical attention if we add a wolf to the rabbit and squirrel. Maybe it is better not to try this and just go home since there are so many ways it can go wrong now or after getting back to the orphanage. You know, things like the wind changing to blow the wrong way like it just did.

The nearest wolf, a young male about a hundred meters away, suddenly put his head up to sniff the breeze. Ugh! The intermittent rain that might have helped hide our scent had quit for the moment. *Change back wind, quickly!*

Too late to get away unnoticed! The wolf lowers his head and gives a low, quiet growl barely heard from here. It alerts the pack of five. Backpedaling out of the brush quickly and quietly to avoid scaring them, we add space between the three of us and the wolves while taking an old rod off its belt loop. Bunnybun and Squiggles will not be able to help if this becomes a fight, the wolves being naturally happy to snack on such prey. But we are not unprepared. The ancient rod, made of plastic and metal, had depended for its power on some corrosive chemicals in a small package. This has been replaced, of course, with a much less harmful power source. With Papa's help we replaced all the corroded parts, cleaned the rest, and rebuilt it with a three-way switch.

We get clear enough to turn around and race up the gentle slope over decaying concrete and scrubby brush toward Sanctuary. The wolves are much faster. Soon, high-pitched chittering is coming from the top of the backpack where Squiggles is alerting us with a mind-image that the wolves are closing in.

This is not going to work! *Stupid Tem! Always getting into trouble.* Well, we have at least brought the rod, not being a complete idiot. *Dear Creator, please forgive this feeble one. Please guide her and help her get her friends out of this stupid situation, which is all her fault! Please make the wolves leave without doing damage or getting seriously hurt.*

We stopped, flicking the power to the first level and turning just as the young male starts to leap at us. Desperately jabbing with the rod, we catch him in the chest. He yips and misses his target, almost instantly regaining his balance. The pack arrives and circles around. *Why are they doing this?* Wolves should run away if they feel threatened. There is a lot of food in the wild, so they are certainly not starving.

We thumb the power up a notch, not impressed with the results of level one. Another chitter and mind-image shows a wolf approaching from behind.

We whirl around and do a better jab, this wolf managing to bite the rod's end and nearly pull it away as it gets a strong zap. It shrieks and backs off, pawing its mouth and rubbing its face in the grass while we regain our balance. The others hesitate. We should be easy prey. Two snacks and a small human should not be able to cause pain. They should be easy prey.

We try to connect with the wolves, sending a picture of friendship. An image comes to us of an old-world place with rusty, leaking barrels and a human with a stick shooting at them. Beyond that image are feelings of rage and confusion, nothing else.

One more level of power is available. We thumb up to it, hoping there will be no need to hurt any of the wolves that much. Surely, they are having second thoughts about this. But no, two come at us at once, from the left and the right.

We swing the rod in an arc, catching one on the face and the other on its belly as it bites the off-side arm. Both scream and back away, reeling from the pain of the shocks and taking the pack with them. We strive to regain our balance, from the one wolf nearly pulling us over and from being in contact as it feels the pain. They back away, turning to go farther east. The smell of singed fur and flesh lingers after them.

It's an awful sound, the pitiful crying of animals in pain. Just awful. We know that sound will be there forever now along with the shared pain stuck in the mind, which will come up from the depths at night and join other memories that crawl through nightmares with the knowledge that we had caused that pain.

This was a really bad idea. Lesson learned. *Think out experiments all the way to the end, without assuming a good outcome.* Seems that more ego was in that plan than usual. Wolves don't think like herbivores like us who just want to get along and not be eaten. Carnivores want to kill, rend, and eat meat. Note to self— stick with herbivores.

What a waste of a day off because of a teacher conference, though obviously we did learn some things.

We regain our composure as a sigh escapes, freeing the disappointment and self-reproach. The arm throbs once. Don't think about it. If you think about it, or look at it, it will hurt a lot more. Change where your thoughts are. What might the next experiment be?

Maybe there's a bison herd nearby. Would they be good friends? That's all we want, after all—friends to fill the emptiness. Oh, and to help the community. Uh-oh, was this actually a selfish thing, not a service thing? Hmm.

We are taught that referring to ourselves as "we" and "us," which I know can be confusing, avoids expressing the vulgarities of "I" and "me" and "mine," which emphasize oneself and not the community.

Anyway, more research is needed before tackling bison. Time to get out of here before the pack decides the meal is worth a bit of pain. And the arm is throbbing. It'll have to be examined and treated. That means the doctor, darn it! Know-it-all busybody—reading people's minds. Actually, more like just reading our character and mood and then diagnosing all too well the reasons behind stuff.

Can't avoid it this time. Too many diseases had surged back after the global collapse. All sorts of germs could be percolating inside the skin. Maybe that's why the wolves attacked. What diseases were in that biology lesson—distemper? Rabies? Okay, another research failure.

It takes an hour to walk back to town, skipping Sanctuary to get the arm treated sooner. Maybe one of those old, polluting cars would be handy right now, but the people of the world are living smarter, and walking is excellent exercise. It gives one time to think. Cars are for emergencies, not for fun.

We step onto a paved street while sending a quick c-fone message to the doctor, hoping to catch him at his office.

"Sorry, he's not here," his assistant replies.

Today is going all wrong. She tells us Dr. Todros is already at the orphanage doing health checks on everyone. He's looking for cold and flu symptoms, probably escorted by Matron. Well, fine. Let's get it all over with at the same time. Bunnybun and Squiggles put their heads down in the backpack as the zipper closes them in.

* * *

The room for the twelve-and-over girls has two bunk beds, one on each side, meaning four of us live there. We're in a small town, with only about a thousand residents, but circumstances have recently orphaned several of us.

The open door to our room reveals Matron Constance and Dr. Todros sitting on Steadfast's bed, waiting. They see us. *Please, Creator, this is a good time for Tem to shrivel up and die, fall into a crack in the floor and die, or maybe freeze literally like the rest of our body metaphorically did and die to be with our parents.*

Dr. Todros smiles, the Matron does not. She looks sad and angry, probably disappointed again.

Matron demands, "Where have you been and what happened to your arm?! Your sleeve is all bloody and torn!"

Looking down, one can see she is right. The sleeve is a mess. Oh, now it *hurts!*

The doctor gently hushes Matron Constance with hand motions then asks if she could "wait outside, please, since this is a small room, and some space and privacy will be needed to treat her injury. Just in the hall with the door open will be fine." He thanks her as she stands to do as he has asked.

"Now, dear Temerity. Perhaps you have been named too well? Please remove your jacket and get comfortable, then tell what happened."

The backpack must come off carefully to avoid jostling our friends. The jacket and shirt have dried to the skin, pulling on the wounds as the jacket comes off and the shirt sleeve gets rolled up. The doctor gasps as he sees what is a nasty bite. He shakes his head, turning the arm this way and that, then quietly asks, "A feral dog?"

Looking down at our knees we quietly answer, "A wolf."

"A WOLF?!" Matron Constance, who has been listening to the conversation, storms back into the room. "A WOLF! Of all the stupid—"

"Matron—" the doctor says.

"Selfish—"

"Matron!"

"Egotistical hubris— "

"MATRON CONSTANCE!" The doctor finally has her attention. "This is not helpful. You must calm yourself and return to the hall."

With a great show of effort, she bottles up her rage and goes back to standing in the hall.

"Now, Temerity," Doctor T. says while choosing certain items from his doctor's bag. "How did it happen that you found yourself near enough a wolf to get bitten?" He begins dabbing at the arm with something to numb and sanitize it.

"Well, it seems logical that someone who can communicate with certain animals should be able to communicate with all of them. Surely, having a wolf as a willing ally—for instance, in searching for a lost child—would be a great help."

The doctor smiles as he works, having somehow found that sincere statement humorous.

"Why is that funny?" Temerity asks.

"It seems you communicated quite well with them. They told you clearly that they consider you food and somehow you told them they were wrong. So, you succeeded in that part. How did you find these wolves?"

"Saw them in the distance on a walk."

"Do you know where they came from?"

We shake our head no and shrug.

The doctor puts in a couple of stitches. "There are a few people who have domestic dogs that can be trained for rescue and such without any danger at all, yet you chose to seek out an animal that would gladly have you for dinner. Why is that?"

This question takes a little thinking, since there are several parts to the answer that are best left unsaid—such as craving to communicate with wild things. Besides, where's the excitement in befriending a domestic, belly-crawling, subservient dog compared to a wild wolf? Also, what's wrong with wanting to create a new family? The safe answer, the one that comes out, is, "We're not allowed to have dogs here."

The doctor runs the skin mender over the arm as he whispers quietly, "Nor rabbits, nor squirrels, yet Bunnybun and Squiggles are getting restless in the backpack. And a wolf would be hardly more welcome than a dog." In his normal voice, he says, "Few adults with many years of experience would try to train a wolf. A twelve-year-old with good intentions but no experience has little chance of survival, let alone success. So, how did you survive?"

We unhitch the rod and hand it to him. He looks at it with interest. "You made this?"

"Partly. It was in an old building. The power pack was badly corroded and had to be replaced. Papa helped, saying at least it would be some protection if walking the wilds was irresistible. Researching it brought up a bunch of similar images, all called "cattle prods." Though why one would choose to shock a domestic animal baffles us. And shocking wild cattle would be suicidal. Unless one were only using it for defense."

He was smiling again. "As you did today."

"Yes." Granted, the image of trying to defend oneself from a thousand pounds of charging bull with a little electric rod was kind of ridiculous. By the time the bull felt the shock one would already be a smudge of mud.

"And where is the old building you found it in?"

"Northwest a couple of miles. Looks like an old farm with some fencing still up, the remains of a foundation, and a stone barn."

"But the prod still worked? The other old tech devices we've found have been inoperable for a long time."

"No, it didn't work. That's why it had to be rebuilt."

The doctor begins dabbing another antibiotic on the bite, gently smoothing it across and down.

"Doctor Todros, a question, if I may?"

"Certainly," he responds.

"Wolves are supposed to run away from people. But these attacked, even before we got close. Is there something wrong with them?"

"Did you get any thought response from them?"

"Just a picture." We describe the scene of leaking barrels and a human shooting a gun.

"Hmmm." He deliberates for a few seconds. "Perhaps you're right. Maybe they were poisoned, or injured, and they blamed humans. A question for you, Temerity. Why so many big words and complex sentences, interspersed with terse responses? Most twelve-year-olds like to condense and simplify, but not to that degree."

Hmm, we notice that the doctor has changed direction. Seems innocent enough to answer, though. "Adults are impressed by big words. They approve."

"And the terse answers?"

"Don't know what else to say."

The doctor thinks about that. One can see it getting filed away under a mental folder with her name Temerity Cruces on it. "You could find a family with dogs and ask to train one, if they would keep it for you."

"Matron C. would not allow it," we say sourly.

"Matron Constance needs more help." He puts the mender away and bandages the injury while saying, "The Counsel is discussing it, but right now she and Dev take care of five infants, three more under school age, plus the older children after school and on weekends. Any parent of only one infant will tell you it's a full-time job to keep them clean, clothed, fed and happy. Please don't be too hard on her. It is not fair that she suddenly has too many children and no time for you. And it's not fair that she does not yet have more than one assistant. We hope both problems will soon be solved."

You see? The doctor is so darned reasonable—and maybe psychic? Or perhaps he just understands people.

The doctor finishes securing the wrap and returns to his bag for something.

Matron C. knocks on the door, looking—abashed? Definitely uncomfortable.

"Temerity, Dr. Todros is correct. This is not fair to you. The others are social and do well, making friends and serving the community together. We know this is much more difficult for you and..."

Oh, good grief! Is she apologizing? What then? Will it be necessary to talk to her more? We like being silent.

Matron continues. "Well, this situation is simply not right, and we apologize for not being more patient."

"Ouch!" A small jab signals the vaccination and antibiotic shot being administered. Probably an extra measure in case the wolves were ill. A good thing that it's a surprise, or it may have been necessary to stop us from running away.

That puts an end to the discussion.

Matron adds, "Thank you, Doctor. We have to get busy now before the shift storm arrives."

"Yes, of course. Thank you for your patience."

Matron leaves suddenly, but her comment alarms us. "Shift storm?" we ask Dr. Todros. "The rain is going to shift?"

"Yes. Predictions are difficult, of course, but it looks like a bad one. A lot of warm, wet air has poured in, as you know from your adventure. A very strong and dry cold front is approaching. Everyone is bringing in loose items and closing their garden domes. Time to be off now. You take care of that arm. Keep it clean and dry." He smiles at the often-spoken words. "And no more wolves!"

"Yes, Doctor. Thank you."

It is necessary to wait a few moments to be sure the hall is clear of adults. Backpack in hand, we walk quickly to the kitchen, finding it empty of cooks. They must be helping with storm preparations. We quickly fill the backpack with dry foods—crackers, cookies, nuts and fruit, all packed in a compartment separate and safe from the sharp teeth of our companions. Two steel water bottles, filled from the kitchen faucet, hang on the outside. Other pockets hold those things we always carry, like a pocketknife, spoon, fork, bowl and a small container of condiments. A quick and furtive trip back to the room adds a much heavier coat and a couple of sweaters to a separate canvas bag.

Chapter Two

Soon, our trio is back on the road headed out of town to Sanctuary. Quite a few people are clearing away anything that might fly or break in high winds. The dome-covered homes, gardens and orchards are being covered over with polycrete segments sliding up from storage to protect them from winds, hail and the sudden shock of large temperature changes. Those who notice our passage wave greetings, so we wave back, not believing the sincerity of their smiles. Why would anyone really smile at us?

Once out of town, away from the eyes of humans, we open the backpack pocket with our companions and their heads pop out. Bunnybun puts her front paws up on a shoulder, tickling our neck with her whiskers. Squiggles snuffles the opposite ear and pats with alternating paws, asking for an elimination break. It's safe from wolves here, about fifteen minutes from Sanctuary. The pack is much farther out and a bit more west.

The companions scurry from the backpack when it lands on the grass. Wow, they both really had to go! Yeah, they were in there a long while, since before finding the wolf pack. The winds are picking up and getting more random now. A large, sunny break in the clouds is coming, warming earth and humid air before the approaching front.

Squirrel and rabbit both casually stroll back into the pack. A short walk later finds us in front of Sanctuary, home away from home, where no other humans are allowed. This is an odd building, made with vertically straight concrete sides on a circular foundation topped with a concrete conical roof. But the peak, or point, of the cone is rounded. Somehow this simple, roomy building has survived since before the collapse.

The rusty metal door squawks as it opens. The hinges have been oiled several times since we found this place, but the damage of weather and old age could not be oiled away.

The interior is dim, without a single window. There are some light fixtures near the roof, but power has been gone a long time. The fixtures now provide nesting sites for several bird species. On the concrete floor are two large machines. A lot of pondering provides probable functions for these devices. The long one—with small wheels up front and large ones in back, a glass-enclosed seat near the rear and a long forward-curved blade in the middle—was probably for scraping the ground. Maybe not farm ground, more likely roads. There is also a very large truck, high enough that one must climb to open the door. It has a back bed that would hold quite a large cargo and seems to be able to lift at the bed's front, which would disgorge its contents out the back.

Opposite these are two large piles, one of sand and one of a mixture of salt and cinders. If it is true that the long machine was for making or fixing roads, and that the dumping machine was for carrying and dropping these piles, then the sand was for traction on the roads and the salt/cinders would help melt snow. Therefore, in all probability, this building used to be for some company or government agency that would take care of roads.

Of course, now these machines are as dead as the lights, and the floor is strewn with bird debris. The sand and salt piles, however, do not seem much decayed. The salt has absorbed some humidity and melted a bit, evidenced by puddles with crystalline salt edges. The sand is strewn about somewhat, maybe by feral cats or raccoons using it to dig and eliminate. It smells damp, dusty and neglected. *Just like me.* That causes a snort of resentment and self-pity.

The seat in the front of the truck is the trio's favorite hideaway. We climb up and open the door.

Squiggles jumps out before we can take the backpack off, romping around the various parts of the compartment, tail wiggling in question marks. Bunnybun is more sedate, gently hopping out and sniffing to be sure no strangers have come around, its ears swiveling to capture sounds.

A small pile of almonds for the former and a couple of greenhouse lettuce leaves for the latter, and we all settle in for dinner—and maybe a nap. It has been a hard day. But before the nap, a check on the weather.

Still munching a lovely, dried peach, we stroll to the door, noting a big uptick in the strength and inconsistency of the wind. A light, warm breeze this way and a strong, cool gust that way— all around, up and down. That could mean serious trouble.

The sunny interval had warmed the old building. Now it is creaking and tapping after the clouds cut off the source of heat. The temperature rapidly chills. We stand there (okay, *one* of us stands there while the other two careen around playing in the bobbing grass) staring blankly at the darkening clouds, breathing in that pre-storm smell, ignoring the gusts that shift hair this way and that.

Suddenly, everything stops. The sounds are gone, the wind is calm, the animals motionless. And then, a distant rumble not varying like thunder, but continuous.

It is visible to the south-southwest, rapidly bearing down on our hometown, a massive tornado of snow, ice and rain, visible only by the debris it picks up and throws about. It is … too big to comprehend. The c-fone emits a warning signal that we don't need, telling everyone to get to shelter immediately.

Squiggles and Bunnybun dash into the building. We throw ourself to the ground at the doorway and on prayerful knees put our hands on the earth, eyes closed, mind deep in the soul, aware of life all around. *Oh my God, oh my God! Please, if Thou wouldst, guide the ground animals deeper into the earth. Protect the animals of land and if they need shelter, please help them to find it. This door is open to all. Oh, and the birds, too, if Thou dost wish it. Also, if it please Thee, please keep the wolves away from the tornado, but don't let them in here. Thank you for your help! Sorry we haven't memorized that prayer for natural disasters, yet.*

A hard, wet splat on the back reminds us to get under cover as huge drops of rain begin to fall. One of the big equipment doors can open, which allows in larger animals. A short struggle is required to unlatch it and push it up.

The taps of large rain and small hail are getting faster. A few birds fly in the big door. Then a doe and fawn run in. A few minutes later, a larger flock of birds of all kinds zoom in and up to the lights. The hail becomes inch-sized, heralding something much worse.

Suddenly, several horses canter in at full speed while the noise of the plum-sized hail pounds the ground outside and on the roof. A few more animals arrive, a bit more beaten up, some bleeding. Several deer, an opossum, three raccoons, and suddenly one more horse. Hail like cabbage heads begins to pummel the roof. The large door crashes down as we hurry to close it, running to the people door to secure that, too.

Having done our best, we retreat to the big truck, carrying Bunnybun while Squiggles scampers up. It takes a few moments, sitting and looking at the various animals, to realize that some need medical attention. Especially that last horse.

Another sudden silence suggests this would be a good time to slam the truck door shut and dive for cover under the steering wheel. Our two companions agree, wriggling up against us as a gigantic boom shakes the building. Nothing can be heard over the scream of the wind. So far, the building holds, the roof is still on—but for how long? Is this a direct hit with the wind wall on the back side even worse? The big equipment doors are on the north side. They will get the worst of the storm's side winds.

But all we can do is wait. Our trio shivers in the dark, hanging on to each other and the hope that heaven is not expecting us soon.

Sometime later, Squiggles pokes a cold nose against a bare face, waking us up. It's quiet. The wind has stopped. We are alive! Praised be God!

There is a lantern in the backpack that only takes a moment to pull out and turn on. Opening the truck door startles a few new friends, but the horses appear glad for the light. The raccoons have taken up residence in the cab of the long machine, apparently having been there before. The possum is also quite comfortable, gazing down from one of the lights. The deer are wary and skittish, grouped together between the salt and sand. The horses form another group, several of them trembling with shock.

One of them, a gorgeous, dappled gray that came in last, is to one side of the group, its head hanging. We go to him first, looking just past him, and ask permission to check his injuries (predators and rivals look directly at prey). He is covered in welts, scratches and a couple of deep scrapes. Hail, especially large hail, can be jagged and sharp, which would make wounds like this. The impact welts are like a whole hive of bee stings on his topline and sides.

Any well-prepared explorer will tell you a first aid kit is vital. However, anyone under fifteen will tell you how hard it is to get or make a good one. We do have a spray for superficial scratches, a gift from Mother last year. That will help on the ones still bleeding. We carefully run gentle fingers over the skull and shoulders of the gray where bones are near the surface. There is a lot of low swelling, but with a light tug on his chin he walks a few steps without limping. The antiseptic spray also relieves pain, helping him relax and give a grateful snuffle in our hair.

We spray what we can on the others, keeping a gentle hand on each horse as we work, telling them how brave they are for standing so still and picturing the injuries to reassure them that none are life threatening. We use up the spray but tuck the empty container into the backpack to refill later.

Now the building. The people door opens outward with a lot of effort but only moves a few inches. As night comes, snow begins falling lightly, glistening in the lamplight. A large pile of hail is slowly fusing against the door, holding it almost closed.

So much for getting to Hopewell's evening Sing. After the big storm, there probably is no evening Sing tonight. Everyone will be too busy cleaning up. We like the evening Sings. They allow us to be part of a group doing something beautiful together without attracting attention to us as individuals.

The big doors are still in place, mostly. The one that was stuck is now dented, causing gaps around the edges. The one that would open is not dented but is stuck.

Well, heck! There isn't any food for all these animals. Maybe water is possible. There are a couple of buckets in one corner and a plastic bowl from under the truck seat. Shoulder against the door—oh, wait, not that shoulder—the arm hurts still. The other arm is better but awkward. The door opens enough to grab some chunks of ice to fill the buckets. These get set out in the middle of the open space. A couple of emergency water-proof hand-warmers from the backpack get dropped into the buckets and begin to melt the ice.

The building is cold after the long winter freeze, though warm enough with the wind blocked. The animals all still have most of their winter coats or downy feathers to warm them up once the shock wears off. The birds, wary of the predatory possum and raccoons, keep to the light fixtures and overhead wires. We'd have to get them some water, too. Hmm.

Climbing the truck is difficult with a water bottle swinging by a belt loop and a bowl in one hand. Leaving the truck door open, one foot reaches to the bed thingy, then our weight shifts over to it while grabbing a handhold on the top rim. Then pull one-handed to stand, drop the bowl into the bed and use both hands to push up and swing a leg over. Bring over the other leg, hop down for the bowl, and figure.

The light fixtures are long and flat on top. One of them is just reachable if standing on the truck roof. The bowl got zipped into the coat to keep both hands free. Then step in a niche here, pull up there, step on the rim, knee to the roof, don't look down, no problem, stand up. No, still don't look down. Look up, at the light fixture. Okay, standing but feeling a bit woozy like the building is moving, water pouring into the bowl. Lift bowl carefully up—okay, not quite as high as it seemed. A small pop in our injury suggests a stitch just pulled out. Bowl is securely placed. Well, unless a bird knocks it down.

Now, sit slowly on the roof while looking at the truck bed. *Not the ground!* The truck bed. Slide from roof to truck bed. Ta da! Whew! Climb down niche in bed, over rim on belly, find footing blind... repeat—find footing blind. Oh, found it, thank goodness. And back into the front of the truck. Hope the stupid birds appreciate that effort. We may have the temerity to seek out wolves, but only at ground level. Ground level is good. And wolves are not.

And now, now that long-delayed nap on the truck seat. Or maybe even a full sleep for the night. Warm coat, Bunnybun and Squiggles curled up against the tummy, and off to dreamland.

Chapter Three

"Don't forget to do the dishes," Coury reminded us. Mom and Dad were gone again, off on another project, leaving Coury in charge. Again.

"And get those vermin out of the house."

"They're not vermin! Well, they are, but clean vermin and part of the family."

"Not part of my family, you freak! Now put them outside!"

"Mom lets me keep them in my room!"

"She left me in charge, and I say outside! They're disgusting! Do you want Mom to know you refuse to behave while they are gone?"

Both of us were red faced by this point, and quite loud. Coury, three years the elder, had size on her side.

"You're not Mom, and you don't get to change our rules!"

"Fine, hand them over and they'll get outside without your help!"

"No, you won't touch them!" Just as both lunged for the animals there was a knock at the door. Coury pointed a reprimanding finger at us as she went to the door. It was the Social Assistance Committee come to say our parents had ascended, caught in a winter flash flood miles from the originating storm. And the world had died.

* * *

We wake up with paws on our face and tears streaming down.

We hate that dream, the memory from three months ago when another shift storm had suddenly turned winter to spring. Coury had decided that raising a younger sister was beyond her, and she had gone to live with her best friend while sending us to the orphanage. We haven't spoken since.

These mornings are the worst, waking up in grief and torment that takes hours to push away. All the dark thoughts, mistakes made, injuries received and given, wondering why our parents found projects away from home to be much more important than their daughters, difficulty communicating with one's own species and their kindly dismissal of this talent with animals.

Well, today there are others relying on us. We wipe our eyes and nose on the torn shirt—it's already trashed, so what's a little snot? Squiggles is whipping that tail around and scratching at the backpack for breakfast. Bunnybun swivels her ears while watching us intently, nose practically dancing as it sniffs, hoping for the same.

Fortunately, enough was packed yesterday to cover several days. Nuts to squirrel, lettuce and grain to rabbit, and dry fruit with nuts to the human. Then it is time to check on the other inmates.

We hold up the c-fone to check the time, finding it is an hour before dawn.

Sorry, Lord. Too little water for proper ablutions, and freeing the others is a priority. Hopefully, it is okay to pray while doing the "work as worship" thing.

The building is much colder than the sort-of cozy truck. If one doesn't mind the crackling plastic seat cover or the smell of mice, it's rather comfortable— much better than the cold concrete we land on after letting the warm air out of the truck. The lantern still has some charge but will need sunlight to recharge for tonight.

The cold air seems to have helped minimize the swelling on the dappled gray's injuries. He snuffles a hand asking for grain. The other horses also hope for food. The water buckets are dry with warm packs still working at the bottoms.

The people door opens a bit more, warmish ground having melted quite a bit of the hail and snow.

We can grab bigger chunks of ice that have melded together overnight. The fresh air coming in is quite welcome. Inside air has become a bit ... excrementy (is that a word? Maybe not.) The inside air smells like a lot of excrement. (Better.)

The machinery door that opened yesterday is still stuck. Our lantern lights the way as we squeeze through the doorway and slip and slide to that big door on the outside. The melded hail has conformed against the door, holding it closed. After a few kicks and a prayer of thanks that the backpack with our friends was not on when we fell backwards, the door looks to be free but still would not budge. A few more kicks loosen the door from the ground. Now it opens, letting all the warm air out.

We slip and slide over the remaining ice lumps back to the people door. By the time we get in, the deer have left, trotting joyfully in their regained freedom. Most of the other critters follow as dawn begins to break. The raccoons, possum and birds prefer to wait for ... something. Whatever. Their choice. Though if the opportunity arises, it would be good to get the gray horse to the veterinarian. Maybe he would follow if he is offered some oats?

Back at the truck, we help our friends down to the ground. When the oat bag comes out, Bunnybun gets excited, standing at her tallest with paws on our leg. She gets a gentle scratching between the ears.

"Not for you, dear. This is for our injured friend."

The horse points his ears forward, his head about level with his topline. Mentally, we warn him, "Don't bite any hands," as one handful of grain is held out to him. He carefully lips the oats in, licking our hand clean. His tongue is warm, pink and very slick, so he is warm enough, not bleeding out internally, and drank enough water. Great.

And at the same time, ick. The slimy hand gets wiped on our pants.

Roger. We'll call him Roger for now, from some foggy association between the name and horses.

Roger looks ready and okay enough to follow us back to town. Bunnybun and Squiggles both choose to run along rather than ride in the backpack. They play tag while racing and leaping in the open field. We head out into the warm sunrise, glad for the clearing sky, fresh air and soft bare patches between areas of ice and snow.

We travel south, keeping away from the edge of the woods in case the wolves have found our trail to Sanctuary. Woods are great for ambushes.

* * *

It only takes about ten minutes for Bunnybun to decide that riding is better. She does not like to have muddy, cold feet. Instead, she wipes her dirty feet on my coat and nuzzles my neck. Squiggles has too much energy to stay still. He zips ahead, then stops to dig or sniff and then waits for us before doing it again, flicking his tail at every stop.

Roger follows and is given some oats every few minutes. He stumbles on ice rocks occasionally, causing us all to halt until his pain lessens enough to continue. Too bad he won't fit in the backpack. If he did, of course, we'd be unable to pick it up.

Finally, tired and a bit sore from our adventures, we are near town. But something is wrong there. People are usually up by this time for prayers in the temple at the center of town. Quite a few of the community members are running around digging and yelling.

Uh oh. Despite the reinforcing and careful building of the town, some of the buildings have been damaged. It looks like people are trapped in the debris.

We put the backpack on the ground, grab Squiggles, and dump him unceremoniously into the pack, zipping it closed to protect both. Looking at Roger, it is suddenly obvious that he cannot put his head down to the grass to graze. Another handful of oats gets him to the edge of town where we find a bird bath that has been emptied, cleaned and put back upside down for winter. We turn it over, wondering how it still rests in place after the storm, and then dump the rest of the oats into it, leaving Roger to care for himself temporarily.

We look around at the clusters of humans, searching for someone … reliable? Trustworthy? Amiable?

Yes, amiable. Not enough of a description, though, as pretty much everyone is amiable. Okay, we are going to have to ask a random person if they need help and hope they do not ignore us.

The nearest group is carefully removing debris from a collapsed house. A man is standing to one side, possibly looking for something.

"Pardon, please, Mr. Crosby. Is help needed here?" we ask.

He looks down at our scrawny twelve-year-old self. "Thank you for the offer, Temerity. We need muscle and a crane to shift this junk. The Duvalls are okay but can't get out of their basement." We all move out of way for three adults carrying away a section of roof. "You might try the eldercare home. They have damage, too."

Hopefully no injuries to the elderly. Surely, their home is one of the strongest. Maybe the storm was even worse here in town. Papa had told us all buildings are made of recycled materials now. Old cities and roads are broken up and the rubble mixed with old plastic and some other stuff, which is then poured over a reinforcing form. It is supposed to be much stronger than any previous building material. How did it fail?

The Home is just two streets and a short jog away. When we arrive, we find more people calling and digging, hauling debris and caring for the injured. The dome over the home has partially collapsed because of the harder winds of the storm's trailing side, apparently rammed by the large tree now lying on top of the debris. Several men are finishing the removal of the tree. Some must have been working all night. Sawdust piles show just how large the tree was, and remnant cross-sections are as tall as us!

Dr. Todros is there, wiping something on the bleeding hands of a nurse.

"Doctor?" We try to get his attention.

He looks around, "Tem, praised be God! We had no idea where you were."

That he would sound so grateful and relieved is a bit hard to believe. Why should he care? But then, we care about everyone, and we are sure he does even more. As a doctor, he kind of has to.

"Is there anything we might help with?"

"Yes, certainly. Do you know Vosh?" He gestures to a child of about seven who sits on a bench under the remaining roof looking terrified as the people around her dig.

"Yes, a little. What is she afraid of?"

"Her parents were late to the shelter. They help run the storm sirens in the Administrative Building, but then wanted to wait it out with family here. We know they got in the door, though not to the basement in time. Would you sit with her?"

Sitting can be done. "Yes."

We take a chair over next to Vosh and sit. There isn't anything to say, so we just sit. After a few minutes, the child looks up but still does not speak, her wide eyes saying all that is necessary. An idea emerges from deep our the mind and becomes clear.

We take off the backpack, glad for the sun now shining fully to warm the town. Bunnybun and Squiggles are both happy to get out of the pack, exuberantly wiggling their whiskers at Vosh. She stares at them, entranced by their proximity.

"Is ... is it okay to pet them?" Vosh asks.

"Here." We nod and put Bunnybun next to her. "This is Bunnybun. She likes to be scratched between her ears."

Vosh gently scratches. The rabbit slowly puts her front paws on the child's lap and over several minutes eases all the way on. We silently thank Bunnybun for comforting the child.

Squiggles climbs up on our shoulder, tapping lightly on our ear. Turning in his direction, we look straight into his eyes and perceive a question asking what is wrong. We picture the child and her lost parents and sense that the people scrambling around us are searching to find them.

Squiggles pats our face, and we know he is going to help search. How do we know? How does he understand? If only we could figure that out, maybe everyone would be able to understand, and maybe we would not be alone. But that is unimportant right now.

Squiggles starts to work. First, he smells the child's neck, and she giggles. Next, he jumps down, sniffing all around the area but finding nothing of use. He goes over to a spot where people are digging and jumps on the debris in front of the rescuers. Several of them are surprised at the vigorous darting of this strangely behaving squirrel. Squiggles rejects their pile, moving to the far side of the damage as the humans resume their digging.

Minutes pass as Squiggles scrambles back and forth across the debris. Suddenly, he stops, digging a bit to move something, then chittering loudly as if wolves were circling his tree. One would almost expect him to throw a nut or pinecone.

The adults briefly glance toward the noise but otherwise ignore him. We pat Bunnybun to tell her we're just going to see what he found. Squiggles still hollers with all his little squirrel voice can manage until we get within a few feet and call his name. He looks at us, patting his front feet on a curtain that is covering some debris. Wait! That isn't debris (well, yes, partly it is).More importantly, it's a leg!

"Doctor Todros! Someone is here!"

While the doctor makes his way around the pile, Squiggles holds up his front legs to show he wants to be picked up, which we do. Riding on our shoulder, Squiggles watches intently as Dr. T. lifts part of the curtain and calls everyone over to help uncover a body.

We wonder if the leg is attached to a live person, and if that person is the girl's parent. It has been about fifteen hours since the storm. Is it possible that Vosh's parents survived?

The adults push us out of the way as they begin the rescue effort. It is annoying to be shoved to the side, though it is done politely with several mutterings of "excuse us" and "pardon." Well, fine. They have at least twice our mass and lots more muscle. They have practice at this sort of thing, and ... are we being resentful of not yet being grown up? Because really, honestly, that was a large piece of polycrete someone just picked up. Granted, it is not like concrete, being much lighter and stronger, but that was a very big piece.

Okay, good. We move back to a sense of gratitude that we kids don't have to do the hard labor. Much better. Resentment is not a pleasant feeling.

"She's alive!" Dr. Todros's announcement is greeted with cheers and applause. Soon, Vosh comes over with Bunnybun in her arms to see what's happening. On seeing her mother's bloody face, she screams and drops the rabbit. We scoop up Bunnybun before she can be stepped on.

"It's okay, Vosh. She's alive," we say. "Dr. Todros will take care of her." We try to comfort the child, but she is hysterical.

We turn Vosh to face us. "Hey, listen, please. Have you ever gotten a scrape or cut that bled a little bit?"

The child nods, snot running down and tears pouring forth.

"It always looks a bit scary when blood leaks out," we explain, "but it cleans up quickly. She's probably cold, and that's why she is not talking or looking around. Give her some time, okay? Here, see?"

We uncover our injured arm, which now has a couple of bloody spots showing. Oops, must have split a couple of stitches at some point. "This happened yesterday and looked really ugly, but Dr. Todros fixed it up. It just leaked a little and is healing well."

We weren't sure about that, but it probably was, and certainly is what the child needs to hear.

Vosh nods twice, eyes widening to follow the stretcher carrying her mother. Someone she knows is helping carry her mother to the hospital and waves to Vosh to join them.

The digging continues. Now that the child is gone, people are talking more, hoping they can find the father.

Dr. Todros stops, looks at us with Squiggles on our shoulder, and asks, "Tem, do you think Squiggles can do that again?"

We put Bunnybun down, take Squiggles from our shoulder and look him in the eyes. In some wordless way we can't describe, I communicate: "Picture the child, her mother on one side and her father on the other. Zoom in on father. Can you find him?"

Squiggles waves his tail twice and we put him on the ground. He dashes back to the pile. This time, everyone stands still to watch the little squirrel. He quickly moves farther into the pile, then back down to a spot where the mother had been found. He sniffs closely then turns to look at us while patting the end of a fallen door.

"Let's look there," someone says.

Squiggles returns to join us, climbing up pants and jacket to our shoulder. The one who spoke is laying down and looking under and around the door. "Yup, he's here. He's moving a hand."

Loud cheers accompany that news. We move out of the way quickly, this time letting the adults have plenty of room to work.

"Temerity, could you come here, please?" Doctor Todros asks. He is over by the bench tending more hand injuries.

We work our way around, then sit again in the chair next to him and wait for whatever it is he wants to say.

"Tem —where... how..." He stammers. "Words are not coming just now. Except for wow! Amazing! Fantastic! How did you train the squirrel to do that?"

Ummm... "Didn't train. We just talk."

"You didn't have a pocket of treats and teach him to find someone?"

"No."

"You just talk?"

"Yes ... It's only reasonable. Sometimes squirrel babies get lost, too, and need help finding their parents. He knew something was wrong and just needed the situation explained, or pictured, so he could understand."

We can feel the doctor looking at us, but all we can do is look at our feet swinging, not quite able to reach the floor. He must think we're a freak, just like Coury does.

"Would it be okay to give you a thank you hug?" Doctor T. asks.

We look up, see him beaming at us, and we nod yes, trying not to burst into happy tears. We get a nice hug! We ask, "You don't think it's crazy... or weird?"

"Crazy? No, it's miraculous. You and your little animal friends have probably just saved two lives and greatly helped Vosh. This is not something normal for most people, but you seem to have the same talent with..."

Someone calls from the freshly uncovered father. "Doctor Todros!"

"We'll talk later, Tem. Excuse me, please"

There is much urgent discussion as the doctor's bag is emptied of item after item, syringes and bandages and such. When they get Vosh's father on the stretcher, we can see that one arm is bandaged and splinted and a thick bandage is on his head. We pet our rabbit friend while saying thanks to God and asking for healing of that damaged family. We also ask that Vosh will not have to lose either parent. It hurts too much.

We get up, both friends already wanting food. Outside the elder home, we see several people have provided a hot breakfast for everyone in the plaza. We take out our bowl and receive a big scoop of steaming oatmeal with fruit. The garden benches here are a bit crowded, so we move behind a planter in a quiet spot that has quickly melted. We all relax and munch on grass or nuts or oatmeal.

The doctor is nice. Scary, but nice. We like him. He talks to us in a good way and listens well. Yes, it is a bit creepy that he understands things that are unsaid, but it's not a bad thing. Just weird. Like the animal talking thing is weird. We wonder what he was going to say before he was interrupted. The same talent with... animals? Same as who? Or rather *whom*, it should be.

Uh oh, Matron C. is coming. She's coming straight toward us. Should we run?

"Temerity! Quickly! You are wanted out at the Dishers' farm. Their son is missing, and Doctor Todros thinks you can help find him." She comes to stand right in front of us so we scoop up our friends and put them in the pack.

"Where do they live?"

"Northeast of town. Go out Harmony Lane. You'll see several people looking for him. Now hurry."

"Do they know where he was before the storm?"

"They said he went out looking for his horse."

"What does the horse look like?"

"Oh goodness, child. What does that matter? Probably the gray one he rides everywhere."

We head off hurriedly, as the Matron had suggested, but in an unexpected direction.

"Where are you going? That's the wrong way!"

We wave back at her as we jog north to find Roger, the gray horse we had left at the edge of town and hoping he hadn't wandered too far.

Roger had traveled a short distance but in the right direction. We try to lead him homeward. Unfortunately, his injuries had stiffened him up while we were in town. He can barely move his head and neck. His shoulders are swollen at the top. Still, he needs to be home for proper care.

We look him directly in the eyes as we do with our friends when communicating. At first, he resists, emanating waves of discomfort. If his bones are broken or cracked, walking him home may be a very bad idea. We ask Roger if he wants to stay here, cold and hungry, or go home to hay and water and maybe a vet with pain blockers.

He sighs, takes a step forward, then another, and slowly loosens up as we head toward his home. We go east, staying along the northern edge of town, both our little friends watching over our shoulders. Roger is walking much better by the time we pass the biogas station where sewage and manure are fermented to make usable gas (mostly methanol). We step off unmelted hail onto clear road, marking the line between the storm impact and the undisturbed side.

Windmills on hilltops become visible before we get to Harmony Lane. When we near a turn to the north, we can hear the discordant sonics meant to ward off birds from the dangerous parts.

Roger is now recognizing the way home and perking up as we turn north. He is leading the way.

The storm must have stayed west of here. There is no hail or snow anywhere. That makes walking much easier as we travel a few more miles north.

Up ahead on a hillside someone shouts at us, or maybe is calling the horse. Anyway, someone yells something but they're too far away to understand what they are saying. Suddenly, several people out in the hills and fields are running toward us.

We stop, our mind freezing with concern, suddenly wondering if they will think we stole Roger or damaged the Dishers' son or something else that might endanger us. Roger keeps going, ears forward, marching toward home.

Two people dash toward Roger.

"Careful! He's injured," we call out.

Roger stops as they block his path. The two individuals slow down, looking Roger over. Then the questions start as more people arrive.

"Where is he hurt?"

"What happened?"

"Where has he been?"

"Have you seen Pov?" This last question is from a rather desperate-looking man, who repeats, "Have you seen our son, Poverty Disher?"

The man's demanding energy causes us to back up a step.

"No, just this horse," we explain.

People are almost surrounding us. Panic starts moving up from our heels to our neck, but a rebellious refusal to flee freezes everything. Now, instinct and conscious mind are warring in our head with conflicting commands.

The man steps forward again as he asks, "But where...?"

A woman steps in front of him, her back to us. She gently says, "Will, give the child some space. She's obviously come from town to return Dusty and doesn't seem to be accustomed to being surrounded by a mob."

The woman turns toward us, "You okay, Honey? Temerity Cruces, right?"

We nod.

"Can you tell us where you found Dusty? That might give us a better place to start looking for Pov."

It's odd when this happens, looking out through our eyes as if looking out a distant window, narrowing what we can take in. The woman in front is clear, and the man can be seen behind her, but everyone else is just movement and blur with a bit of muttering.

"Sure," we say, "but first Rog—uh, *Dusty*—needs attention. He was the last one into Sanctuary and got hit by some very large hail."

The woman called out to someone. "Justice—" But clearly the person she had summoned was already looking Dusty over. "Good. Justice takes care of all health needs of our animals. So, can you answer the question now?"

"Yes. There's this old building roughly west-north-west of here. It's like an almost-dome with ancient road equipment in it. Dusty was the last animal to make it inside, and we waited out the storm there."

Another person said, "That's about ten miles from here. If Pov went that way, we're not even close."

The woman in front of us replies, "Let's get some horses saddled up and head out west." She turns back to us, "Will you show us where this Sanctuary is?"

We could hardly say no. Dr. Todros had told us we might help them. "Sure. How is Dusty?"

Justice is going over him with a portable bone scanner. "He has a few cracks in his withers, but they're small and should heal up. Must have been a huge chunk of hail."

"It was. Size of cabbages."

That simple fact caused muttering all around.

The woman asked, "Was it really that bad?"

After our nod, her attention turned toward town. "Did it hit Hopewell badly?"

We gave another nod, but that seemed to require more explanation. "Some buildings are damaged, people trapped in shelters. A giant tree bashed in part of the elder care home."

The woman had gone a bit pale, as had several others. She leaned back, almost as if to get away from the bearer of bad news.

"Juney." Mr. Disher put a hand on the woman's— Juney's—shoulder. "You can't go rabbiting off to town. We have to find Pov!"

"*You* have to find Pov. You and several others. And take Micky. Those rogue wolves are off in that direction. You know we all love Pov, but he is just one person, and town has many. The rest of us can go help in town. If we're not needed, we'll meet you at … what did you call it?"

"Sanctuary."

"Good name. Pardon our manners, my name is June Nuvo. Pov is my nephew. This is Will, or Mr. Disher, Pov's father. Justice, you go with them in case Pov is hurt. Let's get some food packed up and move out."

Chapter Four

We find ourself herded along the road with the searchers toward the farmhouse dome we see on the next hill left of the road. The small amount of conversation was all about planning the rescue and what might be needed in town, leaving us to trudge along mostly in silence.

Actually, there are several domes almost like a neighborhood at the farm. We assume they're for the other farm families and their equipment. The largest one must be the Dishers' home. However, on arrival we see it is more of a communal building with a large, open room on the ground floor. There are several tables with a kitchen at one side with an open hearth and racks of pans hanging from the ceiling. Maybe the Dishers live upstairs? Or have a small house like everyone else?

Several people go straight to the kitchen to make a meal for everyone. We go to a sparsely populated table and sit down at the end. Soon, wonderful smells are wafting around the room.

One person puts a satellite map of the area on a large wall screen, zooming in and out to fit the farm on the right side and Sanctuary on the left. On the right side is the dull green-tan of early spring. The left side is patchy tan and white. Between them, the dividing line is straight as a ruler, as if they are two different maps separated by season.

There is a lot of grumbling, gesturing at the screen and glancing at us, as if these folks needed visual confirmation to believe what we had told them. Justice, the almost-vet, comes in a few minutes later, glances at the screen but walks on as if he had expected what it was showing. Much to our surprise, he sits rights across from us.

"Wanted to thank you for taking care of Dusty," Justice says. "He'll be fine in a few weeks."

We nod, wondering what to say.

"Saw the signs of antibiotic spray," Justice continues. "You may have saved him from nasty complications."

Umm... "Glad to help."

Justice smiles in understanding. "So, there was a lot of him to disinfect, and it's likely you used up whatever spray you had."

We take off the backpack to pull out the empty spray bottle, keeping our friends inside but putting the pack on the bench. What a relief for our shoulders!

Justice takes the bottle and shakes it. "Yup, empty. Are your pets house-trained?"

"Not pets—they're friends."

"Ah, beg your pardon. If they won't make any mess, you could let them out to stretch a bit. If they are coming with us to search, they could be in there a while."

We stare at our friends for a moment, asking if they want to go out now or later. They communicate "later," taking themselves out of the bag to explore the room. We turn back to Justice, who is staring at us.

"You can talk to them. Not like verbal talking, but with your mind."

Wow. Hearing him say that is so uncomfortable, but nevertheless he continues, "It's okay. I can too. Sorry for the fps," (first-person singular) "but this is very individual. That's why I take care of the animals. I get these nudges about what's wrong, what to look for. Doesn't work as well as your ability seems to."

Just then the food arrives on the serving counter. Everyone gets up to fill a plate, returning to their same spot. Justice gestures for us to join the line. When we get there, June hands us a carrot, saying, "This is for your rabbit, and here's a pile of shelled hickory nuts for the squirrel."

We stare at her, astonished, but manage to thank her. Bunnybun responds to the carrot thought and quickly hops over. Squiggles is so immersed in his game of jumping from windowsill to floor to the next windowsill that he doesn't notice the food until we stare at him. Then he dives into his pile of nuts.

Between bites of lunch, Justice asks, "Would you introduce your friends?"

We look at him curiously, wondering why he wants to meet them. Maybe just because he likes animals?

"Bunnybun, will you say hello to Justice?"

The rabbit looks up from her carrot, then sits up, and waves both front paws at him before going back to her carrot.

"Squiggles, you too. Will you—?" Squiggles does not wait for the rest of the question. He bounds onto the bench, then to the table, landing in front of Justice. The squirrel looks at him and holds up a front paw.

We explain, "He wants you to get closer so he can look in your eyes."

Justice, being quite tall, scoots back to give himself enough room to lean forward, putting his elbows on his knees to get his face down to squirrel level. Squiggles steps forward a bit, then places both front paws on the man's face, looking right into his eyes.

Everyone in the room is riveted on Justice and Squiggles with occasional glances as us. *Great, we're the weirdos in the room, again.*

Squiggles takes an unusually long gaze at Justice but finally breaks it, pats him on one cheek, and returns to the nuts on the floor.

We return to our lunch until June says, "Justice, what in the world did that little guy tell you?"

Justice sniffles, his eyes a bit wet. "Well, June... don't know that it can be put into words."

"Was it about Tink?"

He nods.

We are SO curious, but this is certainly personal for him. Everyone else apparently understands, so we wait, eating everything on our plate, even the horrid home-pickled beets. It's food, after all.

The door opens and a small group enters. One of them says, "The horses are saddled and ready. Seven for town, three packed for searching. Micky is tied to Sunrise."

These things obviously have meaning for the others, but we have no context to understand.

The newly arrived people head for the food while the rest take their plates to the sink for a quick scrub and then go outside. Justice waves us to follow, which we do after scooping up our friends.

The horses are hitched to a rail outside a half-buried dome. I guess that this is the stable. One of the horses has a gigantic dog tied to the saddle on a long rope.

We stop. Justice waves us closer, saying, "No worries. This is Micky, Pov's favorite dog. Don't put your friends down in front of him, but he won't hurt you."

We get closer, offering a hand for Micky to sniff. He finds the smells very interesting, trying to move around behind us in his excitement.

"Micky, leave it," Justice commands sternly.

The enormous dogs stop and sit.

"Good dog."

"Have you ever been on a horse?" Will asks us.

"No."

"Don't talk much, do you?"

"No."

"Okay. We'll put you up and adjust the stirrups—these things hanging here. We'll lead you so you won't have to worry about reins and giving directions, okay?"

We nod.

"Swing your right leg over the back of the horse," Will says as he picks us up by the hips. That is... well, awkward. But we're in the saddle now. The view is different from this sightly increased height. It isn't scary, though, since we are sitting securely. Justice and Will change the stirrups, shortening the straps to bring them up within reach of my feet. When they are high enough to stand up on, the men make sure they are even and secure the strap ends.

The rest of the gathering are riding out toward town as we ask, "Is Micky trained to search?"

The men both put their left foot into their left stirrup and stand up, swinging the right leg over and shifting the saddle a bit. Justice answers, "Nope. Not a bit. We're just hoping he'll try to get to Pov if he gets close enough to smell him."

"Do you have something of Pov's—clothing or something else—that smells like him?"

Will looks at us, then at Micky in a speculative way. He rides over to a nearby building, dashes in and comes out quickly with something in a cloth bag.

Justice says, "That thing on the front of the saddle is called a saddle horn. Hold onto it and lean forward a bit as we take off. Lean back when we slow down. Try to squeeze with your knees to be more secure, but don't kick or squeeze with your feet."

That was a lot of instruction to take in.

Will returns to his horse and encourages it to move quickly toward the west. We start at a walk, letting the horses warm up. After maybe a kilometer, Justice says we are going to speed up to a lope or gentle canter. "Rock with the horse's motion forward," he explains, "and backward to lessen the motion of your upper body."

We take off and—wow!—that makes enough wind to blow our hair back. This is great! Our horse follows well, and Micky has no trouble keeping up. He is in front enjoying the run.

We check on our friends after a while, noting their absence on our shoulders. They are both hunkered down in the backpack, not really liking this fast pace.

Soon after that, we slow to a walk again. Then our curiosity wells up and refuses to be quashed.

"Justice, would... might..." Why are there so many words in the head that refuse to come out?

He glances back, "Go ahead."

"It's personal."

"Okay."

"You won't be offended?"

"Probably not."

Hmmm. "Tink."

He glances back again, and the smile is big on the visible side of his face. "Tink. Short for Tinkerbell, a tiny magical person in an ancient tale. But this Tink was a flying squirrel, tiny even when fully grown. Dad found him when I was maybe ten years old. That seems about right. Tink had fallen from the nest when he was too small to survive without his mother. Dad found signs that the nest had been attacked, and Tink was injured.

We nodded in understanding, appreciating that a squirrel was rescued.

Justice continued. "Our parents decided saving Tink would be a good exercise in empathy and responsibility for us kids, but the others weren't that interested, and he bonded with me at first sight. We were best friends for a long time."

Justice went quiet for a few minutes, but finally asked us, "How did you come upon your friends?"

We thought about how to answer that question. "Squiggles was first. We—I—we were sitting under a tree having snack. It was two years ago when it was so dry during the summer. We poured water into our bowl to rinse it and he came down the tree asking to lick the bowl. We put more water in and he drank. Just to give him more time we sat for a while, and he drank more. When he was done, he sniffed at the backpack, pulling out the bag of nuts. Then he just moved in."

We noticed Justice smiling as his head bobbed with the movement of his horse.

We continued. "A few months later, Squiggles came back from a run very upset and made us follow him to some brambles. Bunnybun was in there. One paw was damaged and there were thorns stuck in her skin. We rescued her and she stayed too."

They continued in silence for a bit, then Justice asked, "When did you know you could understand them?"

"When Squiggles asked for water," we explained. "There aren't many animals in town, and out here they usually disappear before someone could get close."

Justice turned in his saddle to really look as us. "You were running around outside of town when you were what, ten years old?"

This is starting to make us anxious. "Yes."

"And your parents didn't object?"

We don't want to get into that part of the story. The bite on our arm is throbbing again. It itches, too. We pull our arm out of the jacket in a way that won't send the backpack flopping around. There is a little more blood leaking through the bandage. Yes, we ripped out both stitches. That means it will scar. *Cool*!

"Whoa, hold up, Will." Justice brings us all to a stop and jumps down. Walking back to us, he says, "Let's see that arm."

Oh—shoot! He noticed the bleeding. Reluctantly, we answer. "Okay."

"When did this happen?"

"Yesterday."

"Stitches?"

We nod.

"Ripped?"

We shrug a maybe.

"That should be re-bandaged."

"It's okay. Dr. Todros took care of it. Pov needs help more."

"Does it hurt?"

Another shrug. "Itches, though."

He goes back to his horse and takes a container out of a saddle bag. He opens a compartment and takes out something small, coming back to hand it to us. "It's a pain pill. Mild, but it should help."

"Thank you."

He puts the container away and gets on his horse, nudging it to a walk.

Will looks anxious to speed up, but Justice reminds him, "We've got to keep the horses fresh so we can get Pov to a doctor after we find him."

We thought he was correct that Pov would need a doctor, if we were lucky. If he hadn't found some kind of cover when the hail started, or if he had been attacked by something, or gotten lost—well, let's do some prayers for healing.

We get through a couple of memorizations, then resort to prayers made up on the spot asking for help. We need it. Pov needs it, if he is alive. His family needs it if he isn't.

We speed up again, zipping across the landscape, continuing due west over mild hills and shallow valleys. We still stay away from wooded areas. We imagine a branch knocking us right out of the saddle and splat on our back on top of Bunnybun and Squiggles. Not a good picture.

We slow down just before the boundary of fallen hail. It has continued to melt, but the large pieces are still the size of fists, some even bigger.

Justice says, "We'll keep to a walk now to prevent injuries to the horses."

It is a fast walk, nonetheless. Justice pulls the rope to bring our horse closer, then begins teaching us how to ride. Squeeze with the lower legs to go faster, lean back and gently pull the reins to slow down. Steer like this, click for speed like that.

We are surprised to look up and recognize the terrain. "Turn north, we announce. "This is the path to Sanctuary. It's just over the next rise."

Wow, that is some really accurate cross-country riding.

Chapter Five

The men quickly check out Sanctuary to be sure Pov hasn't moved in since morning or something. Maybe he'd dragged himself in there bleeding. Who knows? So, they check it out while we are stuck on the horse because we don't know how to get down. Fine.

We shrug the backpack off and bring it around. Our friends put out cautious noses, wondering if it is safe to look around. We hang the backpack on the saddle horn and try to copy the men's dismount. Swing the right leg over the back of the horse—ow! Stiff legs. Then loosen the left foot from the stirrup and slide down to the ground. Splat! Neither leg is working. What the wahoo is up with that?

Will suddenly arrives and gives us a hand up. "Sorry, we don't have time for many breaks or we'd stop more frequently. Can you continue?"

We nod, but waddle over to the backpack and take it down. Stiff-legged, we move to a nearby bush patch where we smaller three can relieve ourselves in private.

With our comfort much improved, we walk back to the horses to find the men gone. Maybe they went around the far side to do the same thing?

A couple of minutes pass before the men come back, as assumed, from the other side of the building. We try to pick up Bunnybun, but she backs up. She and Squiggles are not thrilled with getting back into the pack for more horse riding. We ask if they would prefer to stay here, maybe in the truck, while we humans continue our travels. They reluctantly climb into the backpack.

Now, to get back on the horse. We pick up our left leg, but no matter what angle we try, the stirrup is too high. Justice gives us another boost up, and oh! The sore legs! But we're back in the saddle.

Will asks, "Do you remember what direction Dusty came from?"

Thinking back, relating the position of the building and the big door, we point, and say, "That way."

Our group moves on, once again at a fast walk. We follow a rough trail through brush finding some large, unmelted hail in the shady spots. The men marvel at the size. Renewed fear for his son pushes Will to go faster, trotting ahead of us. Justice calls him back, reminding him of the danger of a hoof landing on hail.

Will slows again. We can see how this trek to find his son is torturing him. It is mid-afternoon now and chances of finding Pov alive are dwindling. After another kilometer, Micky stops, sniffing the air. The horses also stop. All of us sense a vague unease.

Suddenly, Micky's head raises up, his ears focusing on something ahead and to the right. Then the hair along his spine stands up. Squiggles pokes his head up, puts both paws on our face and chitters. We get a picture of wolves.

A low rumbling comes from Micky as the horses shift nervously. We say, "It's the wolves, the ones... (We almost said the ones from yesterday, but no one else needs to know about that fiasco.) The ones that are usually farther west."

And then, an eerie crooning sounds pierces the air with other voices joining in.

Will tells us in a choked voice, "They have something cornered."

Justice unhooks and drops the rope to our horse. He shouts, "Stay here!" Both men then nudge their horses to full gallops across the mostly muddy ground. Staying here is a great idea, having had a bit too much of wolves yesterday morning. Unfortunately, our companions forgot to tell our horse to stop following and the reins are out of reach as it bolts from a standing stop to a gallop.

We grab the saddle horn just before the sudden motion throws us almost over the raised back of the seat. We hang onto the horn as a couple of stumbles nearly send us flying over the horse's head. The speed alone is terrifying, the destination is terrifying, and the loose rope occasionally tripping the horse is terrifying. We try using the word "whoa" to slow the horse down, then pry a hand from the horn and put it on the horse's neck, repeatedly thinking "Stop! Please!"

Finally, the horse slows down, giving us the chance to grab the reins and pull back gently to slow it even more.

Now we are down to a walk, and we can breathe again. But what happened to the others? We spot them off to the left still going full speed after a couple of wolves racing up the tree line. There is a pile of boulders next to the forest edge where the wolves were. Something is moving in the trees, blending with the shadows and dry grass.

A quiet human voice carries on the breeze from the other side of the boulders, "Help... please!"

We ask the horse to go around the rock pile and find a small cleft facing the tree line near ground level. This is an ambush. The clever wolves had sent decoys to distract the riders, then the bulk of the pack can attack the prey at will. Not that they knew we were coming.

Maybe it was happy accident for them rather than a plan. Either way, we were now between the wolves and their prey.

We force our abused legs to get off the horse and hold us up, taking the electric rod from its loop. The horse immediately bolts away from the danger.

Okay, we can do this alone. A sporadic popping comes from the direction the men rode. Hopefully, they are not hurting the wolves. Then again, these are very dangerous animals that are not afraid of humans. But they are part of the system of nature, keeping wild populations in check.

Why is this so difficult? We, humankind, are supposed to be stewards of nature. But nature is so violent. Why was it made that way? Well, probably to keep everything in balance, to prevent wild swings of populations. But—it is SO violent.

These thoughts are wonderfully distracting as we back up into the cleft, careful not to step on the boy in there. Yes, it is Pov. We'd had several classes together by c-fone. I can see his legs are a mess, and the rest of him does not look much better.

Large chunks of hail are piled in front of the cleft where he must have pushed them after the storm. A small pile remains farther back between boulders, an arms depot for keeping the wolves at bay.

We holler at Pov. "Hi, Pov. Temerity Cruces. We have basic zoology and biology together. Can you stand?"

"Hey. Yes. No."

Okay, that was extremely succinct. A slight sound makes us turn around to check the entrance. Shadowy movement in the woods continues. We grab our c-fone, tap the "all hands" tab to send a message to everyone within twenty kilometers, tap out "911 wolves" and add our GPS point before clicking SEND.

The wolves have decided it is safe to come out. They move silently, heads low in a hunting posture, and begin walking past the entrance, checking for the vulnerability of the new occupant. A few minutes of this with no negative results emboldens them.

The first two come at the cleft together. We already have the rod on full power, sad to have to cause them extreme pain.

Several pings come from the c-fone, but there isn't time to even look at it.

The snarling wolf slightly in front gets a jab of the rod in the chest. Screaming horribly, it twists around to get away, blocking the other wolf.

Naturally this makes the situation very complicated, with one thrashing around and the other one trying to get in. We manage a solid poke at the second wolf's neck while it tries to bite its companion. It also screams, but only backs up, letting the first one out.

Oh, yes. This wolf is emanating negative emotions. In fact, this is the young male that first went after us yesterday. Okay, wolves can be resentful and carry a grudge. Good to know.

This wolf is growling continuously, pacing side to side at the entrance, eyeing the rod as the only thing between him and a feast.

Meanwhile, Tem is not feeling much temerity. More like exhaustion, emotionally and physically. *Creator, could you please strike this wolf down so we don't have to?* We probably can't even hold the rod up much longer. Thankfully, adrenaline keeps us standing and aiming the rod at the wolf.

Suddenly he dodges to our left and tries to duck under the rod, but we are able to jab him on his side near the shoulder to keep him from getting through. He backs to a safe distance again, limping on the leg nearest the jab. The muscles around his shoulder are shaking with spasms. He waits a few minutes for the weakness to subside, paces some more, then begins to hunker down for another attempt. He is not growling this time, just judging his next move.

He stares at us, sending an intimidating picture of us as food. We are intimidated but still keep the rod up hoping Will or Justice or Micky will arrive and remove the danger.

A purple figure suddenly runs past the crevice into the woods. Several more of these figures follow, all seen peripherally since we have to keep our attention on our assailant. What the heck? Are these figures real or are the purple spots meaning something more dangerous is imminent?

Another figure suddenly appears at the crevice opening, instantly aiming and shooting the wolf. The figure spoke in a woman's voice. "Franklin Eyarty. Are you okay?"

Umm, no. And what the heck is Franklin Eyarty?

"Yes," we say, "but Pov isn't." We look down at the bloody legs we are standing over.

"Okay, an ambulance will be here shortly. You are safe now and can put down the weapon."

Weapon? Oh, the rod. We turn it off and let the tip drop, still too wary to put it away or let go of it.

Franklin Eyarty (was that her name?) stays at the entrance, apparently guarding us. That's good, so far. We can get a good look at her now, at least from the back. The purple she and her companions wear is armor from boots to helmet. And they have some sort of long guns.

We wish we all had access to something like that.

The wolf on the ground twitches a little.

"Um, sorry, is he dead?" we ask.

A weak voice behind us says, "Still here."

We turn to look at him and reply, "Sorry, the wolf was intended. Just to know if he's still a danger."

Franklin, still facing the woods, says, "He's tranquilized."

"What will happen to him?"

"Once they are all rounded up, we will sort out the people killers for euthanizing then tag and release the rest. We will try to figure out what caused their rogue behavior.

Sadness at such a loss.

We suddenly remember Will and Justice. "There are two more people out here. They rode off after the wolves that were attacking Pov."

Franklin turns quickly, asking, "Which direction?"

We point north, "Along the edge of the woods."

Franklin begins mumbling into her helmet, giving directions to her team. We can't participate in that, and we do seem to be safe with her on guard. We turn around, careful not to nudge Pov.

"Hey, Pov. Still awake?"

"No."

He sounds more distant, though also surlier. "Where are you hurt? Besides your chewed up legs."

He opens one eye, looking up with incredible exhaustion. "Fell from the rocks. Busted arm. Probable concussion. Cold and hungry. But thanks."

Maybe what had worked with Vosh this morning would help him. "Do you like rabbits?"

No response.

We take off the backpack, set it carefully next to his feet, and try to take out Bunnybun. She refuses to be removed, immediately noticing the wolf lying close by. Okay. We get out several warm packs and start them up, putting one in each of Pov's armpits under his jacket and one on his chest over the heart. Then we squeeze a water-proof warmer into a water container, add two glucose tablets and a tiny electro-lyte pill.

With the lid back, on we shake the container until it feels warm, then uncap it and nudge Pov to take it. There is no point in getting out the dried fruit until he is awake and rehydrated enough to chew it.

Neither of our animal companions is interested in food with a wolf so close. In fact, they are hunkered down in the bottom of their compartment and not even lifting a nose to sniff.

Fine. Lunch feels like a very long time ago, rather than only a few hours. We take some snacks out. The fruit gives some badly needed energy, and the nuts fill in with bulk.

Pov has emptied the water and is holding the container up for more.

"Sorry, but only the one was left. Help should be here..."

The quiet hum of a hover car getting near comes over the rocks. The view out of the crevice is suddenly blocked by a car with a hospital logo. It quickly settles to the ground. Three people get out, one of them being Dr. Todros.

We yell "Here! We're in here!"

We suddenly realize there isn't enough room for a doctor or attendant to get to Pov with us in the way. We grab the backpack, step cautiously over the wolf and step outside just as an attendant arrives at the crevice. Dr. T. grabs the wolf by his back legs and drags him outside.

We say to the attendant, "Wolf-mangled legs, broken arm, head injury."

He looks at us like we are stating our own obviously incorrect pains, so we point inside at Pov. He nods and dashes in.

Dr. Todros comes around the ambulance at that moment. "Temerity! We've been so worried! Are you alright?"

How should we answer that? Does he mean physically, which requires a "yes," or emotionally, which is an emphatic "no"? A shrug will have to suffice.

The doctor comes right up to us, takes our hands in his, and says, "Now, what did I tell you this morning? Hmm? No more wolves. And what did you do? Rescue a wonderful young person from that very problem. You are a marvel."

Oh, jiminy! Tears well up and are soon soaking the doctor's shoulder. Sobs and snot and drool all mix together as he holds us in a gentle hug. Yikes!

Dr. T. pulls a handkerchief out of a pocket and hands it to us. We pull back a bit, still dripping like spring thaw on a warm day, and point toward Pov.

The doctor guides us away from the entrance to let the second attendant in, then goes back to help, saying, "Please don't go anywhere. We have things to discuss later and need to look at your arm again. But right now, Pov needs help more."

They take in some sort of special lift to get Pov on a stretcher without doing further damage. His arm has been splinted already when the stretcher comes out. He looks a little more alert, handing us the empty water container with his good hand.

"Thank you," he tells us.

"Glad to help."

One end of the stretcher fits into a track on the back of the ambulance. The responders press something that lets down stretcher legs to hold up the other end, then the three medical people go to work on their patient. Various things are applied to his legs, a vaccine is given, his head is checked with a portable scanner revealing several cracks in his skull and a concussion, as Pov had realized.

There must have been some pain killer in the shot or leg medications, allowing him to relax and open his eyes wide.

"Dr. Todros?"

"Yes, Pov. It's okay, you're going to be fine. We need to pick up a couple more people, and then we can finish up with you at the hospital. Okay?"

He started to nod, but immediately stopped and simply said, "Yes."

"Temerity." The doctor looks at us. "Would you please ride along in the other seat? We may need some more help."

"Sure." We get in, glad to be in a warm place. The doctor hands us a new water container, warm and tasting of fruit juice with medicine. Oooh, it's so good going down that we drink most of it and ask for another. The second, however, is plain water. Fine.

The attendants get the stretcher in and locked in place quickly, run around to their doors and jump in. It takes only two or three minutes to get to the next stop.

Chapter Six

When we arrive at the next stop, the sight out the window nearly stops our heart. Micky is obviously dead. The horses ridden by Justice and Will are both bleeding, one standing and one on the ground. Franklin and her friends had already been there and two of them were still standing guard over the fallen men. Will is moving, Justice is not.

We open the door as soon as the hovercraft stops, and run to the horses, knowing three people with medical training are available to help the men. The standing horse has several minor injuries to the legs, needing only disinfecting. The other is grunting in pain—three legs with minor injuries, one quite bad. One of the purple people calls for us to get back in the car, explaining that "the area is not safe yet."

But it's a lot safer than half an hour ago. Had it really been that little time?

We walk toward the downed horse, hoping to calm it and ease its pain. When we get close, however, it begins to panic, trying to stand.

"No, no, don't hurt yourself," we mentally croon. "Easy now, we're only here to help out. You're safe, well-protected by the people in purple. We just want to help you and the other humans. Peace, dear one."

An image comes of wolf fangs biting into its back leg, then holding on and ripping. Waves of pain almost overwhelm us.

We get to its head and sit down next to it, slowly stroking the worried face. Eyes roll in concern, but it no longer panics. Its breathing slows, eyes no longer showing their white rims. We ask if we may look at the injury.

The horse lets out a sigh as a positive answer.

The leg is a mess. The wolves were trying to destroy the hamstring and had nearly succeeded. The tendon shows whitish through the rips in the skin. We move around the horse's hind quarters to stroke its back, sending an image of its leg and letting the horse know it will be able to stand up, just not yet. The saddle is still on, so we unbuckle the straps and let it slide down, then gently pull the thingy strap out from under it. Next, we unsaddle the standing horse, which sighs and grunts in gratitude. We leave the bridles on in case they need to be led somewhere.

At the ambulance, uttering barely audible exclamations, Will is being loaded next to his son. The responders continue to work on Justice. He will not be able to act as vet this time. Maybe he and the horses will heal together.

We are still rubbing the downed horse's back when a snuffle and shove make our heart jump again. The second horse is asking for attention. We rub its face, giving it love and reassurance.

A few minutes later, Dr. Todros walks over. "How are they?" he asks us.

We look at the standing horse, "This one has minor injuries, but the other one was almost hamstrung. The tendon is still connected, but the leg is badly mauled and terribly painful."

"Okay. Pov's family is sending a hover transport to pick them up. And that seems to be them, now." He is looking south, nodding toward a boxy vehicle coming their direction. It is long and can surely hold several horses.

We ask, "How are Will and Justice?"

The doctor seems to be looking for an answer but changes the topic back to the horses.

"Do you think you can this horse to stand?" he inquires hopefully.

"Maybe."

We tell the standing horse that help is here, first picturing the boxy vehicle and then rubbing the animal's face. We do the same with the downed horse, asking if it can rise on its own. It thinks a moment, moves the leg a little, and shows doubt. Well, maybe the transport has something to help.

When the truck pulls up, June jumps out, asking the doctor for information on her brother and Justice. Another ranch hand exits the passenger side and comes over.

"Will is going to be fine," Doctor T. explains. "Justice is in good hands and will soon be at the hospital. Pov is badly injured but should be able to mend well."

"Pov was injured? But he is found, obviously! So no need to ask more. Apologies, Doctor, this has been quite an unsettling day."

"No need for apologies, Ms. June. We are all a bit unsettled. Now, do you have a way of lifting this horse?"

She looked at the downed horse with his mangled leg. "Oh, my Lord! That may never heal right."

We interjected, "It will! It just needs treatment."

June has only now noticed us. "Good God, I had forgotten about you, child. You have my sincere apologies."

Umm. Several responses all come up at once, crowding each other out and resulting in silence, so we nod thanks.

"Yes, we have a lift, but the horse will have to cooperate with getting the sling under and around. It will come so near the injured leg we may be unable to do it without getting hurt ourselves."

"It's okay," we tell her. "We can help."

June looks at us strangely, perhaps recalling what Squiggles did at lunch. "Right, then let's get the sling out."

June and the ranch hand walk to the back of the truck and take several minutes to set things up. Then June maneuvers the transport so the rear is only two meters from the spine of the downed horse.

While she is doing that, we explain to the horse what is going on and keep it calm as the hover trailer settles. The crew swings out stabilizers from under the transport's sides, put down a ramp at the back and bring the sling over. This is basically two wide strips of very strong cloth set parallel with a bar holding each set of ends.

The standing horse walks itself right into the transport, choosing a narrow stall and basking in hay and a lot of fresh water.

June shows us how one end of the sling has to go under the horse's midsection before they can attach the cable to the lift.

We ask, "Do you have something to put over the bar so it does not hurt him to roll over it?"

Lej, one of the crew, says, "A good, thick blanket should do the trick."

Lej brings that out, and we tell him, "He's going to roll toward the truck, but we need to help him.

Then someone can put the bar right next to him and he can roll back down over it."

Lej says, "Uh, sorry, but the back legs are too dangerous to help him roll with."

Yes, thrashing is a strong possibility.

Dr. Todros asks us, "Do you trust him not to kick us?"

We ask the horse and get an answer. "Yes," we say.

"Okay, let's help him roll."

Dr. T. and we take the back legs, the others take the front, and we slowly lift. The horse shifts a bit, careful not to kick anyone (though the most-injured leg is shaking). He turns his head and neck as far as they will go in the right direction and manages most of the roll himself.

The sling and blanket are quickly placed, shoving extra sling material next to the rod. For this roll we all stay out of the way, knowing down is harder to control than up. The horse looks at us and we tell it to go ahead. It rolls its legs down and continues as far up on its belly as it can, again groaning in pain—but it is enough. The sling is under him! June pulls the sling bar to take up the slack on the back side while Lej grabs the cable and Dr. Todros throws the other bar over its top side. In just a minute or two the horse is carefully lifted, then is standing and being assisted into the transport.

The other horse munches as it gladly submits to having the bridle replaced by a halter and tie rope to keep it more stable as they drive. It seems happy to be in a safe place.

June and Lej close the back and lock it, waving as they jump back into the front seats.

We nearly faint as they drive away. Communicating with anything is always tiring, and there has been a lot of it today. Now that the various emergencies seem to be over and the adrenaline has long burned out, there is little energy to stand up with.

The ambulance is long gone, back to Hopewell with the three patients. The horse transport has left. No cars or other vehicles can be seen nearby. We've walked this far from town before, but just don't want to face it at the moment.

We ask Dr. T., "How do we get home?"

"The Franklin ERT have a vehicle just over the hill. One of them promised to wait for us." He begins walking.

So that was the name of the group, not one person.

"What does ERT mean?"

"Emergency Response Team."

Oh! That makes perfect sense. The next town west is Franklin. It's so incredibly obvious in hindsight. Does Heartville, the closest town south, have an ERT? Do we? We had never noticed anyone in armor before.

Chapter Seven

Crossing the peak of the hill we can now see a white vehicle with purple accents. Dr. T. says, "The ERT is a new initiative from the Global House, hoping to soon have one in every town. Franklin is the first in this area, since they have the largest population. We all have emergency teams, but these are more specialized with specific training. It would be nice to have some of that armor, eh?"

He smiles at us, and we have to smile back. Yes, it would be very nice.

"Temerity—well, we're almost there. We can talk later."

We look at him, wondering what he keeps wanting to talk about. It must be a long talk since it does not seem to fit into a short walk, and it must be personal since he keeps delaying it in public.

The ERT vehicle has ten seats—we count them when entering—five on each side with an isle down the middle, but only the first three are taken. The front two are for the driver and the navigator. The third seat holds the person who guarded us at the crevice. She looks much more human with her helmet off, much less intimidating. Maybe it would be okay to ask questions.

Dr. Todros beats us to it. First, he introduces himself and us, learning her name is Trust. Then he says, "How is it that your team thankfully happened to be so close when Temerity sent the 'all hands' message?"

"We've been trying to track down this wolf pack for several months. Farmers and others have reported losing animals to them, and they've been seeing them come right up into farmyards and gardens. Then a family was attacked on a picnic. "They were able to tell us the direction the pack went. We've been searching for tracks for two days, finally finding signs just before we got the 911 message."

She looks at us, "That was good thinking, sending the emergency signal and GPS location."

We gave a sigh, wondering what to say. Oh! "Thank you." But there was so much more we could've said.

Trust asks, "Do you actually talk to animals, Temerity?"

We look up, suddenly nervous.

Dr. T. reassures us "You can tell her. She won't laugh."

Warily we answer, "Yes."

"That's a very important skill. It must have been hard to fight off the wolves with your pain stick and then hear them scream."

That was not a good topic.

Trust continued. "I didn't mean to upset you. You showed ingenuity and bravery. You kept the wolves at bay with just an electrical stick, sacrificing your peace to protect someone else."

We had many thoughts but no comments.

"We need people with many different talents. Maybe in a few years you can join a team."

Oooh, that would be amazing, but "How did you know?"

"Saw you talking to the horses. And you have two furry faces peeking out of your backpack." She smiled, though whether at us or at our companions was hard to tell.

We ask, "Why do we have this 'talent'?"

She smiled warmly, "Everything is connected."

And speaking of companions, it was nice of them to come out of hiding. We put both hands back to pet them, getting responses of nervousness. They were not over their terrifying experiences yet. We could all sing that tune together.

Our c-fone pinged—I'd forgotten about that. Probably would have about thirty messages. We go through them, clearing them out as we finish reading each one. Most of them are responses to the emergency text and therefore obsolete. A couple are from adults concerned about us, one of them Dr. T. The final one is from Matron Constance, telling us to get home as soon as possible—or sooner. Our sister is missing.

Too many emotions collide at once causing a freeze-up. Doctor T. notices the change in our expression and reads the message over our shoulder.

"Oh, dear. This day just will not end. Temerity?"

We don't know what to say, so we continue to stare at the c-fone. There is nothing left to think with. No grief. We had lost Coury months ago when she gave us up. Resentment is not helpful, so being glad she's gone is not acceptable. Fear is... well, it's all used up.

Dr. T says, "Temerity, you must be very conflicted right now. This is normal and healthy. May I tell you some assumptions?"

We nod yes.

"You are completely worn out by all the people talk today, plus the emotional and physical toll of all that has happened. Now your sister has disappeared, the sister who you admired growing up but who dumped you in the orphanage when your parents were swept away. I'm wondering—what will you decide to feel? Anger, resentment, worry, love?"

We thought, then answered. "Almost. Skip the admiration. She always made fun of our talking to animals. Said one had to be an animal to understand them."

"Ah, that explains much about your interactions. She wanted to grow up like her friends, with service to the community, not being stuck at home to take care of her little sister every time your parents went on a research trip. Your parents were wonderful people, but we all have flaws. They did not understand just how hard life was for both of you, nor how resentful their older daughter was becoming, nor how unable she was to understand you. "So once again you suffer for the flaws in others, not for your own deeds. Despite all that, your sister loves you."

"She does not."

"She does, but she does not know how to say it or show it."

We look up at him, convinced he is finally wrong.

"You do not believe this," he responds, "but it is true. You can only prove it by finding her and asking for yourself."

He sees this is not convincing us, so he tries a different approach, "If the person missing was unknown to you, would you overcome your current condition and have the courage to do one more rescue?"

Humph. Yes, that would be different. It would require a huge sacrifice to get the energy going again. But if it is worth doing for a stranger, how can we refuse doing it for family? Of course, really, strangers are family too. *God, where can we find the ... whatever, the stuff we need to do this? Where is the energy, the love this one has for anyone, and any animal, that she should have for her sister? Where is the forgiveness for abandonment? How can we find the strength to do another search today?*

We look up and see Trust watching us in her peripheral vision. Dr. T. is also waiting for an answer.

This is hard, but we say, "Okay."

Doctor T. asks Trust, "Do you have any stim drinks? It's going to be a long evening."

"Can junior youth have them? They are a bit strong for her size," she replies.

"One is for your friendly doctor," he smiles. "Half of one is for the junior youth who has had a parade of trials since before the storm hit yesterday. She needs the help."

"One and a half stim drinks coming up. Actually, this one will drink the other half. We've never had to put down animals before. It was... was hard. Even the ones that were badly injured beyond saving were... they were difficult. Those that were taken back to the facility at Franklin hopefully will be able to be released.

"They may have been poisoned."

Trust replies, "We are pretty sure that is what happened to some of them. A guard at a toxic waste site reported several wolves in there among the leaking barrels. He scared them off with a rifle, but the toxins cause irreparable brain damage much like rabies."

Ooh, that explains a lot. We start sipping our stim drink, the first time we've ever been allowed. It works quickly, bringing energy levels almost up to normal. Hey, with this stuff we could rule the world! But who would want to?

Dr. Todros cautions us, "The stim drinks last only an hour or two. When it runs out you will be even more tired than before—so be ready."

Chapter Eight

After a short time, we are distracted by our arrival at Hopewell. There is little activity now. Perhaps the rescues are done—except for one more.

The three Franklin ERT people come with us to help with the possible rescue. We find Matron Constance and several other people waiting for us in the plaza next to the temple. Several teen girls look weepy. We know they are Coury's closest friends. One of them, Joyous, is the one Coury moved in with. Her parents are also here. They look worried.

Resentment is not productive, we remind ourself. Nor is jealousy.

Matron C. walks toward Dr. Todros and greets him. One wonders how she has no time for older kids but has been away from the youngers all day. This question is not resentment, but puzzlement.

"Dr. Todros, I'm so glad you are here with Temerity. We have been running ragged looking for Courage, but we've seen no sign of her."

Dr. T. asks Joyous, "Do you have any information on where she was last? Did she mention some place she might go?"

Joyous has puffy eyes that have shed all their tears. "No. There was such a rush as the storm came. She was helping cover the greenhouses, but then we were separated and..." She sniffs.

Another girl adds, "We searched Joy's house, the greenhouses, the main orchard and the temple gardens. Nothing."

"We tried calling," Joyous says, "and tracing her c-fone, but nothing happens, like it isn't working."

"Is there a place she goes frequently?" The doctor asks. "Maybe some place she feels safe or needs to protect?"

Joyous shakes her head but the question has sparked an answer.

We say, "Home."

"Which home?" Matron C. asks. "With Joyous's family? The Home for the Elderly?"

"No. Home, our house—where our parents lived. She would want to protect it, and everyone else was probably busy. Nobody lives in it now."

Several of them nod agreement.

Matron C. says, "That's a very good possibility. Temerity, would you lead the way, please?"

Ooo, a *please*. That was nice! "Sure. It's three blocks east." This stim drink is great!

The streets are almost completely clear of hail, snow and whatever debris the tornado had dropped. The sun is setting as we walk away from it, turning the eastern sky brilliant colors from white through yellow, pink, magenta and purple. It's a beautiful gift, and probably everyone is getting their own message from it. We get several, the biggest being a reminder that after crisis comes victory. Today has been quite a crisis. Hopefully something good is coming.

With the setting of the sun the temperature drops rapidly. If Coury is still alive, she would not be for long.

We turn up the third street and stop. If she had gotten this far, she did not have time to close up. Windows and doors are blown out, curtains wave in the breeze. She would have gone to the garden first to close that dome and protect her plants.

We look at Joy and her parents and say, "Check the garden."

They head in that direction as we go across the street to a neighbor's house.

Dr. Todros asks, "Temerity, where are you going?"

"Coury objects to vermin," we reply,

He lets further questions remain unspoken, and we are grateful.

We knock on the door. Ms. Benningham answers, surprised to see us. "Temerity, it has been months," she tells us. "Are you okay? Do you need something?"

Yes, she's a talker, but tries to keep it to a minimum. "Do you still have Gypsy?" we inquire.

"Yes. Why do you ask?"

We think a moment about how to reply, but she won't understand. We just say, "Would it be okay to borrow her for few minutes? Dr. Todros will stay with us." Because the whole town trusts the doctor.

She looks thoroughly confused, but then Dr. T. assures her, "There will be no danger. You may come along if you wish."

"We are just sitting down to dinner, but Gypsy already had hers." She turns toward the inside of the house and calls, "Gypsy, come here, girl. That's a good baby! Here she is."

Gypsy, a small, feisty and energetic dog, is handed over to us. We tell Ms. Benningham, "We'll have her back shortly. Please say hello to Mr. Benningham and Jubilee for us."

A few more courteous remarks are required before we can carry Gypsy across to the abandoned house. Streetlights are on, and when we get inside, a few working lights show the damage. The house's lighter contents are strewn about and many are gone, having been sucked out the windows. Even heavy furniture has moved, creating obstacles and heaps in what used to be throughways.

We go upstairs to Coury's room, remembering things we have tried to forget—good times that hurt to think about and bad times that plague us. We go to her bed and place Gypsy on it, then we gaze into her eyes.

First, we get a greeting, and happiness that we remember each other. Then a question— does she remember our sister? Smell the bed, Gypsy, this is her bed.

She sniffs around on the bed, getting stale but still distinct smells of Coury.

Then we ask if she can use that smell to find our sister. She sniffs around more energetically, digging here and there to bring up more scent. She turns her lovely dark eyes to ours, confident that if she comes across that scent, she will recognize it.

We take her downstairs and ask her to search. We trot with her through the rooms, getting no sign of success.

Then we get to the utility room, the one with the controls for home protection and dome cover. Gypsy gets quite excited, barking and bouncing. She runs to the back door, which we open for her.

Out she zips, losing the scent trail on the ground. It has rained and snowed since Coury went through here, but if she went to the garden, her scent may still be present. We cross the yard to the dome ten meters away and then open the door, seeing Joy and her parents searching there. The garden dome is closed, protected by the polycrete sections. We let Gypsy in to run back and forth as we asked her, but she finds nothing.

Hmm...

Dr. Todros has been quietly following us, but now he asks, "What do you think?"

Well, good question. "She was here in the house. Gypsy smelled her at the dome controls. She would have come out to check on the dome, make sure it had closed completely. Then she would go back in to close the house."

We call Gypsy, who comes merrily. Turning back toward the house, we seek what might have happened.

Searching in our soul for guidance, we try to think like Coury. We have secured the plants we love and obsess about. We come out, look around to see... maybe we see the storm coming, and ...

Not working. Gypsy, meanwhile, is romping about in the dark. She suddenly lets out several high-pitched yaps, throwing her head back with woo-woos in victorious celebration.

Dr. Todros runs over, but we do not. We don't want to see. She didn't get under cover in time. She could not have survived. But then, we think, how did she not get sucked into the tornado?

There is an outside access to the basement shelter. Is that what Gypsy is barking at? The ruckus is in that area.

Dr. Todros holds up Coury's c-fone from under the remnant of a huge piece of hail and calls for help. Joyous and her family are already arriving. Gobs of hail have frozen together on the outside access holding it closed. Heavy furniture had probably blocked the inside access. So, Coury is fine. Dropped her c-phone in the storm and it was smashed by hail. Good. Mystery solved. No point in waiting around.

We go pick up Gypsy and take her home, thanking the Benninghams for letting us borrow her. They ask questions, but we suggest talking to Dr. Todros.

We walk a block, let out Bunnybun and Squiggles, and when they are ready, we go home. Maybe there will still be some dinner.

* * *

It's hard to wake up. There's no reason to, but someone keeps shaking our shoulders. Go away! Can't say that. Large sigh, giving in to the inevitable. We turn over and open our eyes a little, seeing Steadfast, our roommate and Coury's friend.

"What?"

"Good morning to you, too," she replies as a mild admonishment. "Dr. T. said you would still be tired this morning—and ravenously hungry. Come on, get some breakfast. Then some people want to talk to you."

That's alarming. "Who wants to talk to me? Why? What—?"

She interrupts, "Have some patience. And some breakfast. No worries, this is a good thing." She takes a step toward the door, then turns back again. "And do freshen up a bit. All those stress chemicals are coming out in your sweat."

"Okay."

We get up, scrub quickly, and dress for visitors. There is still some breakfast, so we pile our plate with almost everything left. Yes, ravenous is the right word. Next, a quick tooth brushing and check for cleanliness. Pack up Bunnybun and Squiggles. And off we go to find whoever is waiting.

They are in Matron C.'s office, but Matron C. is not. Dr. Todros is there, casually chatting with Coury.

This is not okay.

Dr. T. sees us and asks us to come in and sit. Fine. We sit facing both of them. Coury has bruises on her face, and one hand is bandaged thickly. There is a box behind Coury that issues small noises infrequently.

We greet them cordially, "Good morning Dr. Todros, Coury."

They reply more warmly, Dr. T. saying, "Good morning, dear Temerity. How are you today?"

Coury says, "Hey, Tem. How have you been?"

We reply to both, "Sore. Busy. And you?"

Coury looks nervously at Dr. T. like she knows this is not going well.

Dr. T. explains, "Your sister and I have been discussing several things, and some of them concern you. The first is that she acknowledges things went badly between you. There were several misunderstandings, and she really does want the best for you. We agree that the orphanage is not the best place for you to live, but also that a fifteen-year-old is hardly equipped to care for a twelve-year-old. Therefore, she has agreed to give up her guardianship of you to me, if you would like to be adopted."

Moments tick by in silence.

"Wait. Adopted? You mean you want to be my parent?"

Doctor T. grins and nods.

Then we ask, "Why?"

"Ah, so many reasons. Partly because I see some of me in you. Our talents are very similar. What this doctor understands in humans you understand in animals, those things that speak from the eyes or body."

Coury joins in, "Turns out it is also similar to my talent. I understand what plants need. This didn't seem like something unusual until moving in with Joyous and working with her parents. They have had me going all around town with them, evaluating plants and soils and suggesting what would work better."

We notice that our shoes are dirty. We forgot to clean them. Noticing our shoes is a distraction, we know, from the shock of what is happening.

Maybe Coury is sorry for trying to throw our companions out, now that she understands a bit. If she apologizes, we'll have to forgive her. Nix that. We are supposed to instantly forgive, which puts us several months behind.

We take a deep breath.

"What other reasons?" we ask. The adoption thing is becoming appealing—having a parent again.

Dr. T. is smiling in our peripheral vision. "We seem to be compatible souls," he explains. "We're able to understand each other better than most children and parents. Also—and this is a logical observation, not a bribe—you can have Bunnybun and Squiggles in our home. There is room for them to run around inside or in the garden. Then there is my medical practice. You have shown great skill at helping a traumatized child with a therapy animal. If it interests you, assisting in such work would be an infinite help. Do you need more reasons?

We hesitate to say it, but... "Will you talk to me? Will you go on trips and leave me?"

"Oh, dear Temerity. We will talk about many things, and you can practice with me how to talk to others. And no, God willing, you will not be left. Doctors work in their community. It is rare that one of us is called to go somewhere else, but if that happens, you will certainly go along."

He stopped for a moment and then looked at us with glistening eyes. "I just thought of one more very important reason. I already love you as a daughter."

Then the weeping begins. We rush into Dr. T.'s arms, eventually looking up to find him weeping too. Then Coury comes over and joins us. She apologizes for leaving us, and she's also weeping. We turn and hug her, so glad to have the good Coury back and let go of all the ugly emotions. It takes some time for us all cried out and cleaned up.

A sudden mewling from the box distracts us.

Coury tells us in a voice rough with emotion, "As the storm was bearing down on the town it felt necessary to go home and close up the place. The garden was safe, and I was turning back to take care of the house when the hail started. Something moved to one side of the yard. I went to see what it was just as the hail came down in plum-sized chunks. One hit the little thing directly... and it screeched."

She picks up the box and hands it to us. We start to open the box as she says, "I went to grab it and then didn't have time to get to the back door, so I went in the safe room access, which was closer. The little thing was tearing at my hand, but we got in and turned on the lights, and then I saw what it was. I knew it was for you."

We stare at the small being in the box. It is a kitten, but too large to be the average domestic cat. It is lying down, bandaged almost from head to tail. It is looking back at us, a little fearful but also curious.

Dr. T. says, "We took it to the hospital last night for some emergency reconstruction. Broken ribs were perilously close to puncturing a lung. There was damage to muscle and internal organs, but we were able to set them on the track to healing right."

Both the kitten and we are listening, but still staring at each other, cat to human to cat. The little animal is beautiful with tawny fur that has brown spots and stripes but a white forehead, chin, neck, and belly. Beautiful, detailed face markings. Lynx or bobcat?

Continuing to stare into the box, we know we must ask another question of the doctor. "So you want to be my papa? How would you like to be addressed? Dr. Todros, Dr. T., Dad, Father?"

Dr. Todros sounds a bit choked up as he replies, "Dad will do just fine. And no, this is not about replacing your papa. You will have time to grieve your loss without someone else taking his name."

We nod in thought. "What shall we call this little girl kitten? She says her name is Rabbit Killer, but that won't go over well with Bunnybun. Maybe... Storm Killer? No, she doesn't like that. Is Storm okay? Yes, she agrees."

Dad (that is so amazing!) says, "Remember that her species does hunt rabbits and squirrels. We will have to train Storm not to hunt your other companions. And you must deal with her being a carnivore."

We finally look up at... yikes, at "Dad." We are revolted by the idea of carnivores. Almost all people are vegetarians. Killing animals to eat is ... yuck! Besides, two days ago we learned not to invest in friendship with carnivores.

Dad tells us, "Pov's family has the dogs. They have to have meat, and the family provides it to sick people in town. They do not raise the animals or husband them, but they do cull the weak when necessary. Surely, they can spare some for Storm."

We nod, glad he understands. Then we look at Coury, who has been very quiet. "What about you?"

She smiles, apparently glad we are talking to her. "Joy's family has offered to adopt your sister. Now the offer can be accepted."

"Will we see each other?"

"Of course! We will not let go again."

We put the box with the kitten down and give our sister another hug. "Cour, would you mind if someone else cares for the kitten? I know two people who are better equipped to take care of her, and who might need her now."

"Sure, but you seemed to want a wild carnivore."

We smile and look at Dad. It's going to take a while to get used to thinking that name. "Divine guidance shows the right path, and that is not the path for Tem."

"Cool—little sister is growing up."

We both smile and snort a laugh.

"Umm, Dad, may we go visit the hospital with Storm?"

"Sure. We have several friends to check on. Courage, would you like to come?"

"Thank you, but no. Time to say 'yes' to Joy's parents, and we will both have a second family. But we'll always have the same first family. Cool?"

"Cool," we answer.

Chapter Nine

The hospital is much busier than usual. There are still several patients with storm injuries, as well as wolf encounters. Vosh hails us and runs out of the room we were passing, insisting we visit her parents and introduce them to Bunnybun. Both of them are doing well, though there are yards of bandages on them.

The next roo we visit has three patients—Will, Pov and Justice, plus a woman and a young girl who must be Pov's mother and sister, since they are seated at his bedside and near Will's. Another woman is next to Justice asleep with her head on his bed.

We thought she would wake with an awful crick in her neck.

Our group is warmly greeted by those who are awake. Ms. Disher looks a bit wan, washed out from a long night of watching over her husband and son. The girl is Tempe, Pov's little sister, about ten years old. Pov is asleep.

Ms. Disher comes over quickly, saying, "Dr. Todros, good to see you." They press hands, then she turns to us. "Temerity Cruces, it is so good to meet you. Might a hug be allowed?"

We nod, putting down the box, uncertain what is coming next. She gives a warm, firm hug, then steps back while still holding our shoulders.

"Thank you so much for helping Will and finding Pov. Without you, we'd have lost both of them. We still might lose Justice."

Dad asks, "He is still not out of danger?"

She replies, "No. They've replenished his blood, closed the holes, put things mostly back together, but he hasn't woke up yet. Maybe another day will get him back on the mend."

Dad talks to Ms. Disher and checks over Pov and Will as the girl watches.

We walk over to Justice's bed, seeing the repairs to his neck, legs and arms. One great gash across his face includes an eye. We know eyes are very hard to repair, medical science not having found the best means yet.

We feel a tap on one shoulder. Squiggles is warning that he's coming out. He climbs up our shoulder and jumps to the bed, checks out Justice from head to foot, then looks at us with a message of 'staying with him for now.'

"Okay," we say.

The little squirrel snuggles in next to Justice's head as the woman suddenly wakes up, sees us, and her face scrunches in discomfort as she puts both hands on her neck.

"Hello," she says to us.

"Hi. You okay?"

"Just a bit stiff. Who's this little guy?" she asks while nodding at the squirrel.

"That's Squiggles. He's going to take care of Justice."

Her eyebrows go up in mild surprise. "Okay." She does not seem to know what to say to that.

We put out a hand for introductions. "Temerity," we say.

"Providence. Nice to meet you." She presses our hand.

We nod back.

Providence tells us, "We have seen each other at Festivals and Feasts, but maybe not ever actually met."

We nod again.

Well, that was not a very long conversation, but we have no idea what else to say. Looking around we see that Pov is awake and chatting with Dad, and since we're feeling insecure again, we take Dad's hand. There are small machines over Pov's legs, doing something obscure.

Pov says, "Hi."

"Hi."

"Thanks for keeping the wolves back. Thought it was over, time to ascend the hard way."

"Almost joined you. If the Franklin ERT hadn't arrived just then, well, you know." Why are the adults watching us? Is it cute—adorable children having an awkward conversation?

Dr. Dad suddenly realizes this is getting uncomfortable. He engages Ms. Disher and Tempe in conversation, drawing their attention away.

"So, how are you?" we ask Pov.

"Well, alive and mostly put back together. They are trying to regrow the missing bits of my legs and having difficulty with it, but the arm is all straightened out and healing."

"Did you hear that Dusty is okay?"

"Yeah, Dad told me. He also said Micky…"

"Sorry, yeah, he didn't make it." We are quiet for a moment, then offer, "Would you like to hold Bunnybun? She's a therapy rabbit." She is after helping Vosh, anyway.

"No thanks, not big on herbivores, except Dusty."

Perfect opening. "Hang on a minute." We get the box with the kitten, setting it on his lap. "See what you think."

He opens the box slowly, wondering what is scratching around in there. When it is open, he stares at Storm and Storm stares back. Suddenly, the kitten starts rumbling in her chest. She is purring at Pov. The boy says, "A lynx!" She manages to stand but is unable to climb out with all her injuries and bandages.

Meanwhile, Pov's mouth is hanging open in amazement. Storm says a breathy, "Meh," causing Pov to close his mouth and carefully pick her up. She snuggles against his chest as if she will never move from him. He tears up and we would have offered help, but Pov's mother was suddenly there holding him.

That must be nice, to have a mother who does that.

Then an arm went around us and we remembered we have a dad!

Dad says, "Come on, we have official adoption paperwork to do." He begins steering us toward the door. "Would you like to remain a Cruces or become a Todros? Or we could hyphenate."

Pov interrupts. "Hey, Temerity—we have a foal whose mother rejected her. Would you like her? Mom says with Justice and... and me hurt, there isn't anyone to raise her."

We look at Dad with great excitement. "Could we? Please?"

He smiles, then laughs, throwing his head back. "Yes, my dear, we will work it out."

Acknowledgments

Deepest thanks go to God, husband T.Mike and friend/co-conspirator Cheryll S. for continuing to push this book to the finish plus editing, story suggestions (sorry, dear, the armored squirrels shooting laser rifles just didn't fit) and huge amounts of support. Gary Lindberg at Calumet Editions has done fantastic editing, very much helping the story and getting the typing right. Of course, the author had to go and do more, so anything incorrect falls fully on said author.

Several others have also given moral support and done some editing, including Carol P., Nancy W. and Bob A. Thank you all from the deepest places in my heart.

About the Author

Jennifer Pollard was born in the state of New Jersey, USA. Her family moved to Colorado when she was eleven, allowing her to spend many hours roaming the empty hills around their home. She retired long ago from executive secretarial work at such places as the Rocky Flats Nuclear Plant and the National Renewable Energy Labs. She and her husband moved to Missouri and started a small, organic apple and vegetable farm. They raised two children adopted from Ethiopia and now live with a cat, three small dogs, and thirteen chickens (though the chickens live outside.) She writes fiction for youth and young adults to give them hope for the future, and historical fiction about great figures in religion.